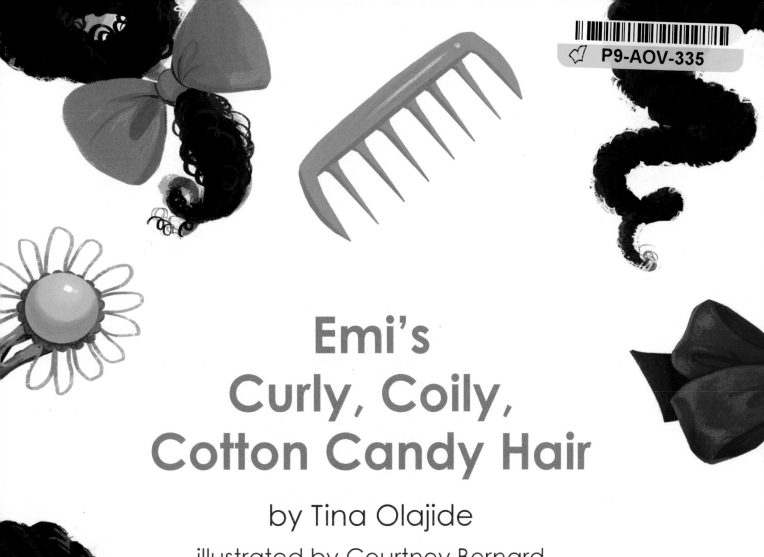

Emi's
Curly, Coily,
Cotton Candy Hair

by Tina Olajide

illustrated by Courtney Bernard

ISBN: 978-1-5031-4494-1

heyemi.com

Hi my name is Emi and I have curly, coily, cotton candy hair.

Parts of it twists and turns
like the slides at the playground.

Other parts are
springy like a slinky.

And this part right here is fluffy like cotton candy.

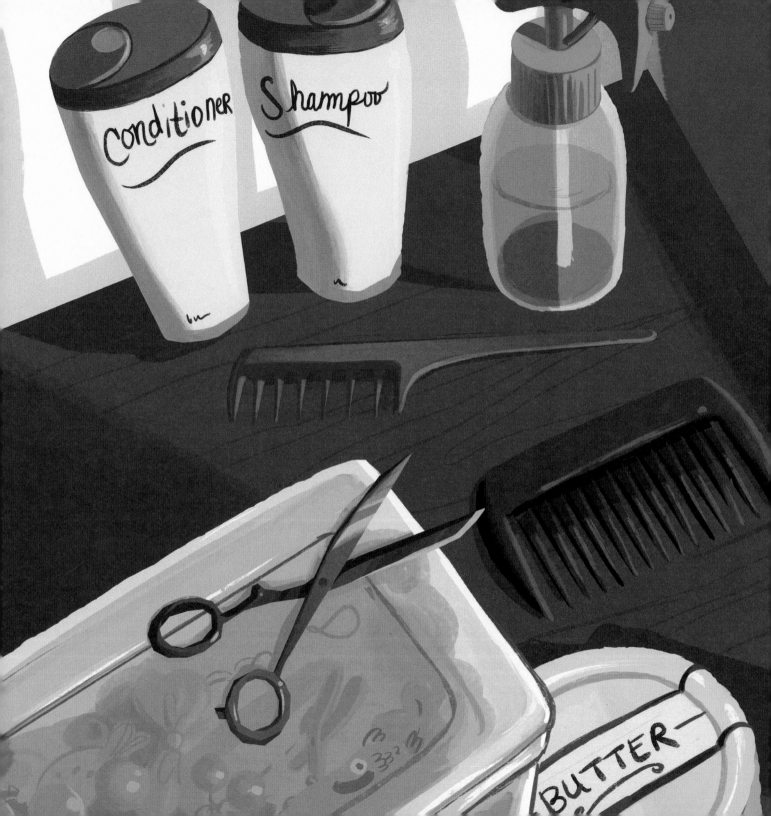

Today mommy is washing my hair and
these are all the tools she needs.

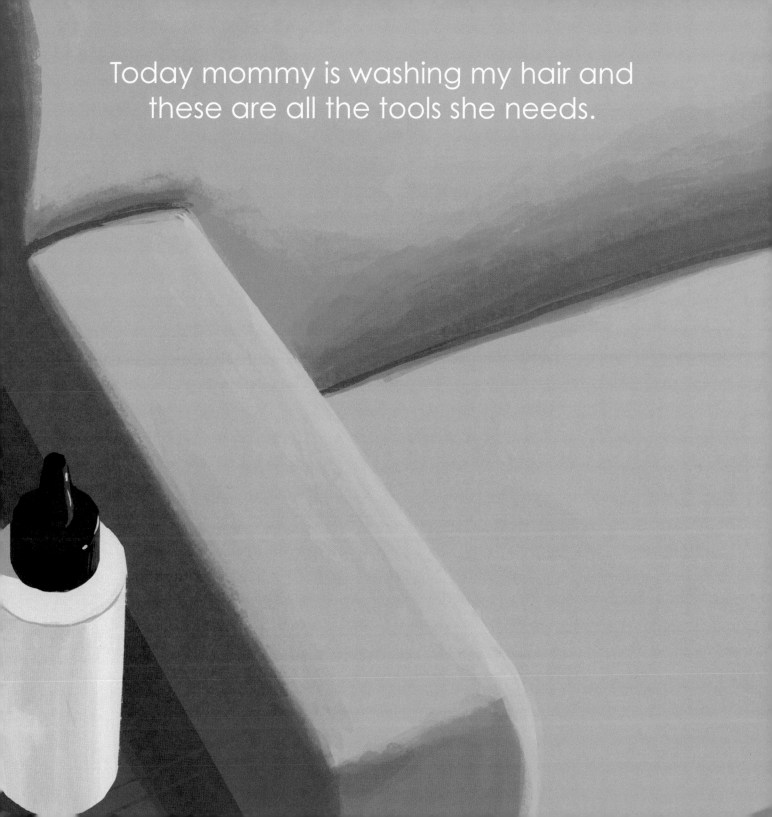

Before she gets started, I
choose a few books
to read.

First mommy has to detangle my hair because
sometimes it tangles into tiny little knots,
just like my jump rope.

Mommy takes her time loosening the tangles and knots in my hair. "Growing healthy hair is easy when you're gentle and patient," said mommy. "These tiny little knots are no match for me!"

The hair at the back of my head is soft, fluffy and tangle-free; mommy calls it cotton candy land.

She parts my hair into four sections and makes four big twists, holding each twist up with a hair clip and off to the bathroom we go!

First, mommy lets the water rinse through my hair. Then, she starts from the back in cotton candy land, unravelling each twist. Adding a little bit of shampoo and water to my scalp, gently massaging it in. She clips it up again.

And then…

1, 2, 3 rinse! Mommy adds a little more shampoo to my scalp, massaging it into each section until it's clean.

And then...

1, 2, 3 rinse!

Next, mommy adds conditioner to my hair
and starting from the ends she combs
through gently with a wide tooth comb.
I like this conditioner because it smells
like vanilla ice cream.

Mommy twists all four sections
and clips each one up again
and then... **1, 2, 3 rinse!**

When mommy is done washing my hair she pats it dry with a towel.

To moisturise my hair mommy unravels each twist
and adds a leave-in conditioner, followed by
whipped hair butter that smells like cocoa.
Too bad I can't eat it.

"How would you like me to style your hair today Emi?" asked mommy.

"This time I want my hair in long twists like liquorice sticks."

"Twists it is," said mommy.

Mommy parts my hair into little sections and one by one she wraps a piece of hair around another all the way to the end.

"Almost done. Which one would you like to wear in your hair?" asked mommy.

"I want..."

"This one!"

At night I wear a satin bonnet
to keep my hair nice and neat
for school tomorrow.

"Your hair looks beautiful princess," said daddy.
"Thank you daddy. Mommy did a great job."
"Yes, she did," said daddy.

My name is Emi and I have curly, coily, cotton candy hair. Parts of it twists and turns like the slides at the playground. Other parts are springy like a slinky. Some parts are fluffy like cotton candy and it's all **beautiful.**

The End.

Made in the USA
Middletown, DE
02 June 2020